RESCUING RHINO

An Orphaned Baby Rhino finds a New Home

by

Judy Maré

Dedicated to all orphaned baby rhinos, who need their story told.

by
Judy Maré

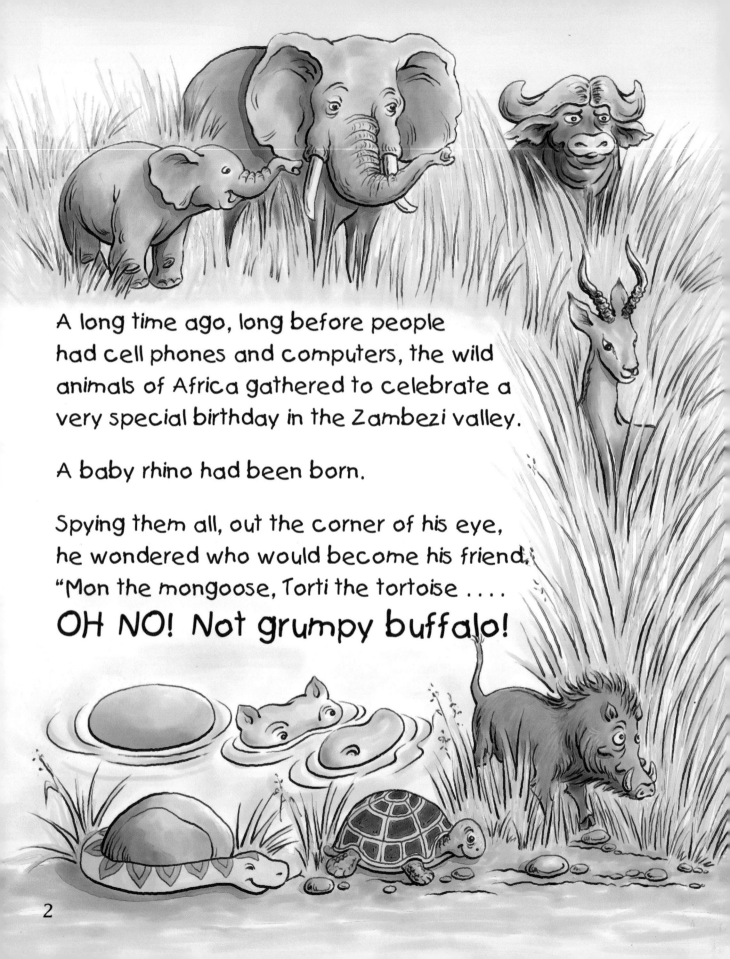

A long time ago, long before people had cell phones and computers, the wild animals of Africa gathered to celebrate a very special birthday in the Zambezi valley.

A baby rhino had been born.

Spying them all, out the corner of his eye, he wondered who would become his friend. "Mon the mongoose, Torti the tortoise . . . . OH NO! Not grumpy buffalo!

But. . . . what was that rumbling noise?
Could it be Elephant's tummy?"

Oh Dear! A gigantic wall was being built across the valley to dam the river. Soon the water began to rise. Every day it rose higher and higher. The hills became islands – very crowded with animals. There was less and less space and less and less food.

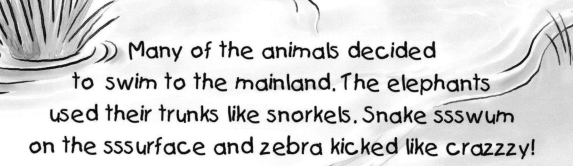

Many of the animals decided to swim to the mainland. The elephants used their trunks like snorkels. Snake ssswum on the sssurface and zebra kicked like crazzzy!

In panic Rhino and Torti watched them leave . . . .

"OH NO! How will we go?

We can't swim like Croc or Hippo!"

Luckily Rupert Fothergill and a Vet
arrived in a flat bottomed boat.
They were part of the animal
rescue called 'Operation Noah'.

Grumpy buffalo was tied to the side but baby Rhino,
Torti and the small critters were given a ride. Once on
the mainland all the others scurried off to find family...
OH NO! What about Rhino?
He was all alone, his *mummy* had drowned.

"Oh this is so sad," said Rupert. "We can't leave him alone for the lions to eat."

"I've an idea," said the Vet. "I'll take him home!"

Meanwhile back at the vet's home, his children were in for a big surprise.

They and their friends were playing in the wild garden, down by the stream – every child's dream.

Some were collecting rocks and stones to build a dam. Rhino saw a girl laughing as she swung over the water on a willow branch . . .

"OH NO! Don't let go!"

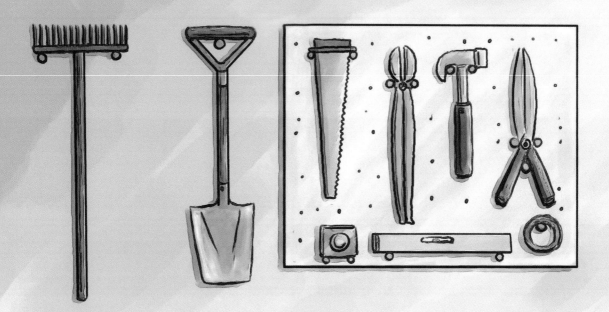

The vet's wife was a nurse and had cared for orphaned animals before. In fact, she had just hand reared a baby zebra.

She made the nervous little rhino a lovely dry bed of straw in the corner of the garage and put a warm light above him to keep him cosy.

The children fed him a little milk, then patted him as they said, "Goodnight." He looked at them as if to say....

"OH NO! Please don't go!"

10

After a few days, the little rhino felt
braver and ventured out into the garden.
All the animals came to say hullo. They were
Moosli and Milo the cows, Ziggy the zebra,
Baasil the sheep, and Rusty the dog.

"What are you and what's your name?" they asked.

"The children call me Ru – pet,
or something like that," he said,
as the children and their friends
clustered round him.

Just then Warti the warthog ran up
to see what all the fuss was about.
He snorted, "You're not a PET!"

"OH NO! You're RHINO, the wild Rhino!"
That made Rhino feel even braver and he gave
everyone a little smile.

13

Rhino was always hungry!

He was still a baby and would have been suckling milk from his mummy. So the vet's wife fed him several big bottles of special milk formula, at least four times every day.

As he got older he learned to suck the milk from a bucket, through a rubber tube – just like drinking with a straw!

Clever Rhino soon realized where his milk was kept and would butt the fridge door to tell everyone when he was hungry....

OH NO! Not the new fridge!

No one could imagine the problem this would cause later!

Rhino's favourite game was practicing being a **wild rhino.**

He rushed around the garden and through the house after Rusty the dog, with Warti the warthog, in hot pursuit.

As he got bigger, Rhino would let the children and their friends climb on his back and try to ride him.

16

"Giddyup!"

"Hold tight!"

The best fun ever was galloping around
the garden, trying to hold on for dear life....

"OH NO! Don't fall off!"
Even Rhino seemed to be laughing!

After such fun under the hot African sun,
Rhino loved to take a cool bath —

a glorious squishy MUD BATH!

When they were tired from all the playing Rhino, Warti and Rusty the dog, could often be seen snoozing together in the shady garden. They also liked the childrens' comfy beds.

OH NO! There's even mud on the pillow!

On cold winter evenings,
Rhino, Warti and Rusty
loved to join the children
in front of the fire,
to keep warm.

Rhino was happiest when they leant against
his big body while doing their homework but ...
OH NO! Something was happening to Rhino!

He was growing
and GROWING
and GROWING.
He was always hungry and the
more he ate, the more he grew.

One day, Milo and Moosli pushed
their way through the hedge into
the neighbour's garden and Rhino
joined them. They were happily
munching her flowers when she
spotted them.

"Oh My Gosh!"
Rhino was now so big he took up all the space in the kitchen.

He had an enormous appetite and would still butt the fridge to remind everyone when he was hungry. One day his long horn went right through the door...

"OH NO! Out you go, Rhino!"

"Rhino, you're growing too big," thought the vet's wife. "Soon you won't be able to fit through the door."

He still liked to sleep on the childrens' beds but ...

OH NO! Something had to go!

One by one, all the beds broke under his weight
and the children ended up sleeping on mattresses
on the floor!

Rhino was so happy with his adopted family.
He had no idea of the damage he was causing.

"I've something to tell you," said Dad the Vet, one day. "It's time for Rhino to go back to live in the wild.

I have made plans to take him to Matopos National Park, where they have built a special enclosure for him."

"OH NO! He can't go!" cried the children but deep inside they knew that going back to the bush was the right thing for Rhino.

"Wild animals belong in the wild," said their Mum with tears in her eyes. "It's where they feel most at home."

The children and their friends were sad to say goodbye
but they were also excited for their special friend.

For a few days, the Vet stayed with Rhino in the enclosure while he explored his new home.

He was excited when he remembered all the sights, sounds and smells of the wild.

The rangers introduced him to Sally, who was a slightly older rhino. She taught him how to survive in the wild and before long, they became best friends.

Free and safe, they roamed the African bush together. Rhino was so happy in his new home!

YES! OH YES!
A very happy WILD Rhinoceros!

Rescuing Rhino Game

Start your game in the Zambezi Valley with the birth of a **baby Rhino**. Join in **Rhino's rescue** and then have fun with him as he **grows-up**. The game **ends** with Rhino being **released** into his new home, in the wild African bush.

To play: You'll need a counter for each player and a dice. Throw an even number to start the game.

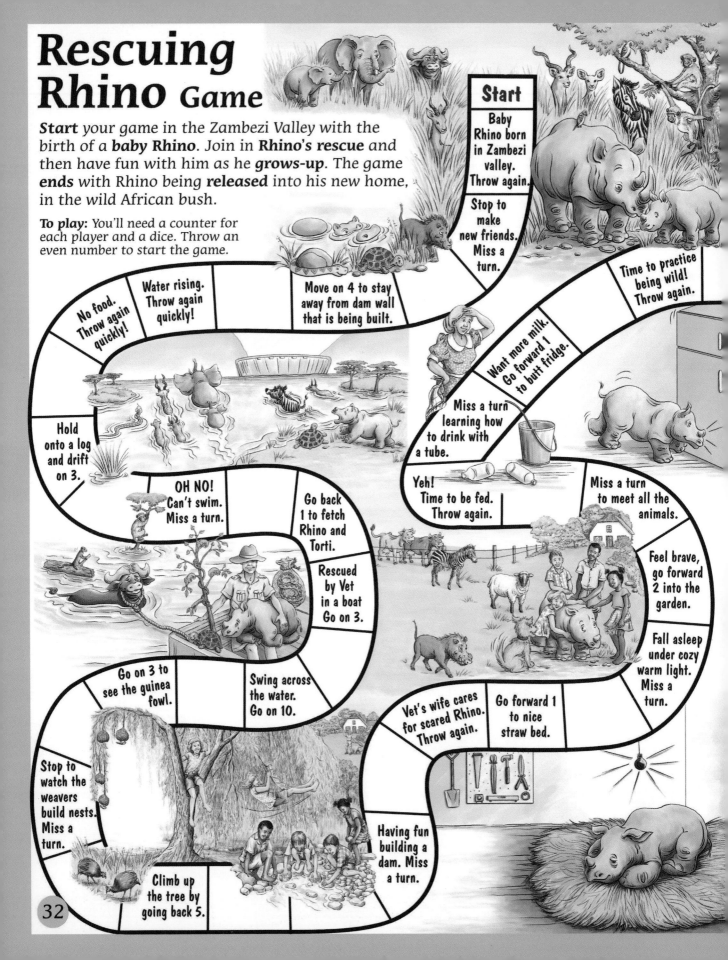

Start
Baby Rhino born in Zambezi valley. Throw again.

Stop to make new friends. Miss a turn.

Time to practice being wild! Throw again.

Want more milk. Go forward 1 to butt fridge.

Miss a turn learning how to drink with a tube.

Yeh! Time to be fed. Throw again.

Miss a turn to meet all the animals.

Feel brave, go forward 2 into the garden.

Fall asleep under cozy warm light. Miss a turn.

Go forward 1 to nice straw bed.

Vet's wife cares for scared Rhino. Throw again.

Having fun building a dam. Miss a turn.

Climb up the tree by going back 5.

Stop to watch the weavers build nests. Miss a turn.

Go on 3 to see the guinea fowl.

Swing across the water. Go on 10.

OH NO! Can't swim. Miss a turn.

Go back 1 to fetch Rhino and Torti.

Rescued by Vet in a boat Go on 3.

Hold onto a log and drift on 3.

No food. Throw again quickly!

Water rising. Throw again quickly!

Move on 4 to stay away from dam wall that is being built.

32

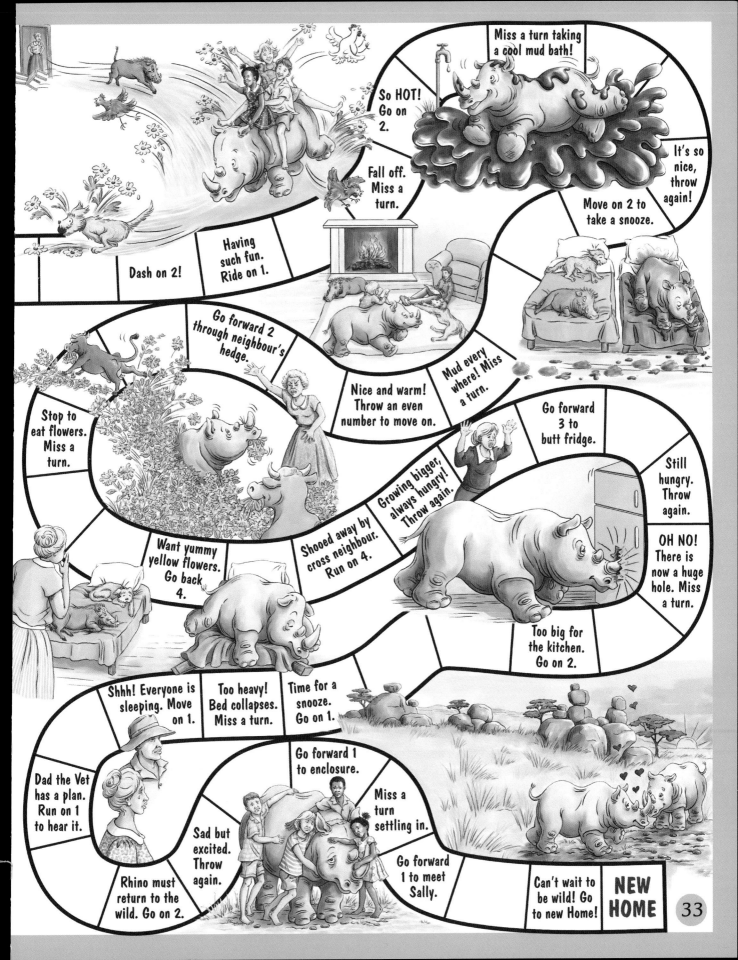

SAVING WILD ANIMALS

Both animals and people **need somewhere safe to live**, with **food** and **water**, if they are to survive and be happy!

Welcome to our world!

People's world

With more and more people in the world, the **towns** and **cities** get **BIGGER** and **BIGGER**.

Kariba Dam, Zimbabwe

Harare, Zimbabwe

All these people **need electricity** and **water** for their homes and businesses. So they build **dams**, like **Kariba dam**, with hydro-electric power stations.

People don't need hunting and **poaching trophies**. Animals are **killed** for these!

Cities, dams, mines and farms **encroach** more and more on natural areas, **driving wild animals from their homes**. To save the animals from dying it's up to **people to rescue them**, as in **Operation Noah**.

Only Elephants and Rhinos need tusks and horns!

Lapwing

Animals' world

This **natural world**, from **jungles** to **deserts**, is **home** to the most amazing **wildlife**. These are just a few of my animal friends that visit this waterhole during the **day**. Many more come at **night**.

Springbok and Gemsbok

Kudu

PLEASE don't poach me!

Rhino

What other animals could be hiding in these pictures?

Fun things to do!

- **Find out** more about Operation Noah and other animal rescues on the internet or at the library.
- **Visit** a game reserve or animal sanctuary and count how many different animals you can find.
- **Try being a game ranger** and play the tracking story game on page 49.

Great view from up here!

Save our world!

Wild animals need **people** to protect their world – keeping them safe with space to roam and feed.

> Help save the rhino!

We don't want to become like the Dodo......**Extinct!**
Here are some interesting **facts about rhinos** that you
may or may not know and why they are in such danger.

White rhino, South Africa

Rhinoceros – The name means 'nose horn' and comes
from the Greek word **rhino** (nose) and **ceros** (horn).
Just called **RHINO** for short.

- There are **five species**: the two from **Africa** are highly **endangered**, three from **Asia** are almost **extinct** and the **western black rhino** from west Africa went **extinct** in **2006**.

Black rhino, Southern Africa

One-horned rhino, India

Sumatran rhino, Sumatra

Less than **40** left in the wild, none in captivity.
Javan rhino, Java

- The **white rhino** is the **second largest land mammal**. They can weigh over 2000kg.
- Rhinos are **herbivores** (plant eaters). They have **poor eyesight** but a **good** sense of **smell and hearing**.

- Rhinos mark out their **territory** with piles of poo or **middens**.
- Females are **pregnant** for **15 - 16 months**. Rhinos are very good mothers and look after their calves for about **3 years**.

- A **herd** of rhinos is called a '**crash**'!
- They can **run** over **50kph** and the fastest person in the world runs at 37kph. So be warned, you cannot out run a rhino!!

- **Rhino horn** is made from **keratin**, the same as our fingernails. It has **NO** scientifically proven uses as a medicine.

Poaching – The number of **rhinos killed** for their
horns has increased so drastically that they are heading
towards **extinction** – **more are being killed than born.**
In **South East Asia** and **Vietnam**, rhinos are
so scarce that the price of horn is very high.
Now **crime syndicates** are paying **poachers**
to kill African rhinos for their horns to sell
in Asia and the east. This causes **horrendous
suffering,** as majestic healthy animals are
butchered for **horns** that people do not need.
If a mother rhino is killed, the **traumatized
baby** is often just left behind to die.

Mother rhino killed by poachers.

Rhinos killed in South Africa

2000	2001	2002	2003	2004	2005	2006	2007	2008	2009	2010	2011	2012	2013
6	7	25	22	10	13	10	13	83	122	333	448	668	1004

STOP rhino poaching before it's too late.

Fun things to do!

- **Find out** what people, around the world, are doing to try and help **Save the Rhino**. Look on the internet.
- **What can you do** to help **Save the Rhino**? See the activity pages for some fun ideas.
- **Draw** and **colour-in** a **Save the Rhino** poster or sticker. See page 46.

Please don't hurt my mommy!

Captive breeding

All over the world, Rhinos are being bred in captivity to **protect** the **species** but it would be a tragedy if they became extinct in the wild.

Mother white rhino and her calf at Monarto Zoo, South Australia.

Orphaned wild animals

I'm an orphan

Wild animal babies become **orphans,** when they are **separated** from their mothers and they can't survive on their own. Their homes or nests may have been destroyed during a storm or their mothers died by **accident** – like our Rhino, but many mothers are **killed** by cars, predators, disease or **poachers.**

Rescue – **Before rescuing** a baby animal make sure the baby is really **an orphan.** Sometimes the parents are too frightened to come and collect their babies when there are humans around. Watch from a distance to see if the mother will return. **All orphaned animals** will be very **frightened** and **traumatized,** whether they are a tiny baby bird, that has fallen from a nest or a baby elephant, like Zongoloni below, whose mother was shot by poachers. They must be **handled quietly, calmly and very carefully.**

© The David Sheldrick Wildlife Trust who rescued and cares for Zongoloni.

Care – If injured, a rescued wild animal must first be treated by a vet. If you can't take it to a wildlife centre immediately, here are the important things an orphan baby needs:

- **Warmth**
  It is important to keep them warm.
- **Fluids**
  They must drink so they don't become dehydrated.
- **Food**
  Feed only if they are calm and the food track is clear.
- **Safe haven**
  They need to be kept somewhere clean, safe and secure.

© Linda Herud

baby vervet monkey

thirsty young rhino
© African Conservation Experience

hungry baby bird
© Blue Ridge Wildlife Center

rescued giraffe calf
© The David Sheldrick Wildlife Trust

Find a wildlife centre that will be able to care for your orphan.

I've got an extra puppy!

Surrogate mother – Some animals will **look after** an **orphaned animal** as if it were their own. This beautiful mother dog let a baby **vervet monkey** suckle along with her own puppies. Sadly the babies **mother** had been **killed by a car**. He was later cared for at a wild life sanctuary.

© Linda Herud

Rehabilitating orphans

We're all growing!

Hand-rearing orphaned wild animals is very different from looking after our pets. They need specialized care.

Rehabilitation – takes months, even years of caring from dedicated people who have made it their job to help animals grow up and return to the wild. They need to know all about how that animal lives in the wild, what it eats and its habits.

Baby elephant orphans being fed formula by keepers at **The David Sheldrick Wildlife Trust**.

Food – The first step to survival is persuading an orphan to feed, but its not easy.
- They must be fed a **formula** as close to their natural food as possible. For example, a baby elephant can't be fed cows' milk, it's not nearly rich enough.
- As they **grow** older it is important to feed each kind of animal the **correct food** and teach them how to find that food. **Predators** (meat eaters) need to learn how to **hunt** and **browsers** taught to eat the correct **leaves**.

Growing up – Every stage is important as most animals, just like children, have to be **taught skills** that they would have learnt from their mothers. Some animals, like birds, grow up very quickly and need less care but others, like the Orangutans, take 6 or 7 years to rear.

- **Nursery**
  They are with a carer **all the time**, day and night as they need a **mother's love**.

  Lone Dröscher Nielsen has dedicated her life to the orangutans on Borneo.

- **Youngsters**
  They still need the love of the carers but are encouraged to **play** and **explore** their surroundings.

  Teaching orangutans to climb and build nests in the trees.

- **Teenagers**
  They become more and more **independent**. They are **taught** what food to look for, dangers to avoid and **how to survive**.

  Lunch in the forest school of **Nyaru Menteng Orangutan Sanctuary**.

REMEMBER! Do not try to raise a wild animal as a pet.

I want to tell you a secret!

Elephant keeper at The David Sheldrick Wildlife Trust.

Special orphan keepers – At **wildlife rehabilitation centres**, all over the world, wonderful **keepers** and **carers** are human surrogate mothers and fathers, helping raise the **orphaned animals**. They need to work in **rotation** so that the animals do not get too attached to one person. Many come from the **local communities**, and they teach their families and others the **importance of saving the wild animals** of the area.

© The David Sheldrick Wildlife Trust

41

Releasing orphans

I'm going home!

When a **hand-reared** wild animal is ready for **release** it can't just be let go. To make sure it has the best chance of **surviving** in the wild many things need to be considered.

Release – The animal's **health** and **fitness** are **assessed**. Only those that have a chance of survival will be released into the wild, others will remain at the santuary.

A cheetah, wearing a **tracking collar**, sets off at great speed after being released by the **Hoedspruit Endangered Species Centre** staff.

Timing

- **Age** – Make sure the animal is **old enough** to cope the stress of being totally on it's own. Must be at least the age they would normally leave their parents care.
- **Time of day** – Release **nocturnal** animals at **night** and **diurnal** animals during the **day**.
- **Weather** – The weather must be **mild** as bad weather will make it even harder for them to settle in or for birds to fly.
- **Season** – Choose a **suitable time of year** when there is **plenty of food**.

Monitoring

- Released animals are often fitted with **tracking collars** or **devices** to be able to monitor how they are coping in the wild. See the cheetah above.

Location

- They must be released in the **type of countryside** that they come from **naturally** .
- The area **must be safe** – where they won't be in **danger from humans**. Often this means it is very remote and hard to get to for the release teams. Such as the orangutan release in Borneo below.

Phew, that took forever!

.....and final release in the jungle where they are monitored to make sure they settle in their new home.

Orangutans go by plane, helicopter and boat.

Are we there yet?

Then a long trek by foot....

Wild animals are meant to be in the wild not kept as pets.

Staff from **Vulpro**, the vulture conservation centre releasing hand-reared vultures.

Fun things to do!

- **Find out more** about the wild life release programs featured in these photographs. See page 62.
- **Find out** if any wild animals have been released near where you live.
- **What can you do** to help release teams? Think of ideas!

Time to spread my wings!

Releasing endangered vultures

Chicks that have been **reared in captivity** are released into the wild to boost the threatened wild populations. **Vultures** are **extremely important** as they eat decaying dead animals, very rapidly – and in this way they keep down the risk of disease for livestock and wildlife.

©Vulpro

43

FUN ACTIVITIES to make and do

You've read **my story**, learnt some **cool facts** about saving me and my wild friends and now it's time to have loads of **fun doing my favourite things!**

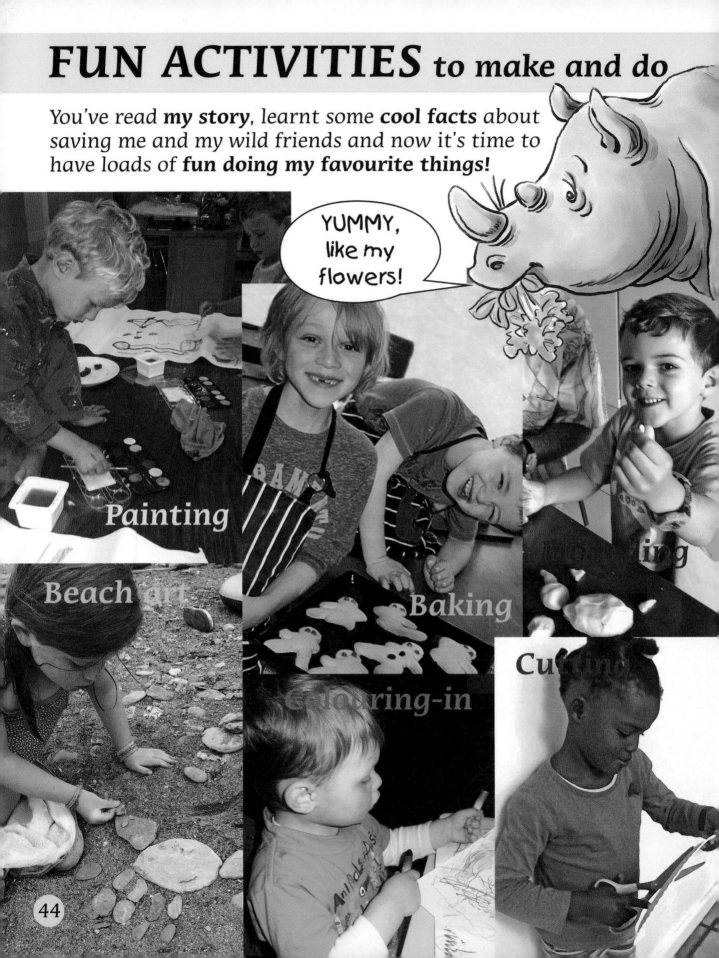

YUMMY, like my flowers!

Painting

Beach art

Baking

Moulding

Cutting

Colouring-in

Save the Rhino

A big thank you!

Copy and colour-in these stickers or create your own. Then cut them out and stick them where they will remind people to help SAVE THE RHINO!

Need: Copied stickers, coloured felt tip markers, paints or crayons, glue, press stick or sticky tape.

SAVE THE RHINO

STOP POACHING

What can you do to help SAVE THE RHINO?

The following activity pages may give you some ideas.

Have FUN!

It's for a good cause!

Kristin and **Maxine** made these stunning fridge magnets to raise funds for *Save the Rhino*.

Beaumont primary school children showing their support for the *Stop Rhino Poaching campaign* at their sports day.

Amazing results!

Alyssa, a grade 2 pupil from Johannesburg, South Africa, has raised over **R170,000** in less than 18 months towards **saving the rhino**. She started the idea herself, selling chocolates, stickers, sweets and biscuits at market days, at school and at events. She has a website and donations page too. Other people have supported her by making toys, jewellery and puzzles for her to sell. Alyssa speaks at schools and has won many awards for her conservation work. **Well Done Alyssa!**

www.savetherhinos.co.za
SAVE THE RHINOS
www.sanparksvolunteers.org

Making tracks

Did you know **animal tracks** are nature's **story tellers** – they tell us **what** animals passed by. **When** it was. **How many** there were. **What** they were **doing** and **where** they were **going**.

> **Need**: 500g bag of Plaster of Paris powder (from a pharmacy or hardware store), paper cups, 1litre water, 2cm high plastic collars cut from cooldrink bottles.

◆ **Look** for nice **clear tracks** that have been made in slightly damp mud.
◆ If it is possible **push** in a **plastic collar** around each print leaving some rim to hold the plaster.
◆ **Half fill a cup** with **Plaster of Paris powder.**
◆ **Slowly add water** to the powder and **stir** the mixture until it becomes **creamy.**
◆ **Quickly fill** the **prints** and **collars.** When the plaster gets **warm** you know it is going to set hard soon – **so hurry!**
◆ **Wait** about **30 minutes** for the Plaster of Paris to **harden.**
◆ **Pull out** the collars and casts.
◆ **Wash off** any mud from your casts.

◆ **Identify** your **track casts**
Look in an animal identification book. **Use** them on the desk **as paper weights** or make an interesting **display at school.**

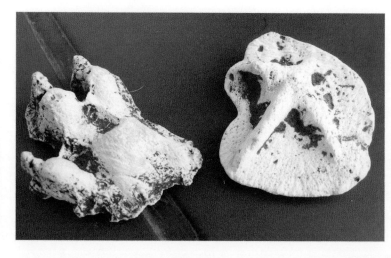

Now it's your chance to **become a game tracker**, like **Zizi**, from Nokana Safari Camp, Kruger.

Study the picture below and **discover** the **story** that the animal **tracks tell**.

◆ **How many** different **types** of tracks can you see.
◆ **What** were the animals that made them as they passed by?
◆ **Look** at how the tracks **lie** on **top** of each other.
◆ **What order** did the animals come past?
◆ **Follow** the rhino's foot prints. Where did he go and what did he eat? Was he a black or a white rhino?
◆ **Follow** the other animals and discover where they **went** and what they **ate**.
◆ Have fun **writing** or **telling** your animal **story** as though you were a **game ranger** or **tracker**.

I hope there aren't any poachers' tracks!

Rhino and ranger biscuits

Bake a delicious **herd of rhino-shaped biscuits** and **decorate** them with **icing** and colourful **sweets**. You can even make a **game ranger** or **animal keeper**.
Use grannies special **ginger biscuit recipe** or your own favourite biscuit recipe, which may have less ginger.

Ginger Biscuit ingredients:
4 tablespoons golden syrup
1 cup sugar
225g margarine
4 cups flour
1 egg
2 tablespoons ginger
3 teaspoons bicarb soda
pinch of salt

Icing: 4 tablespoons butter or margarine, 1 cup icing sugar.

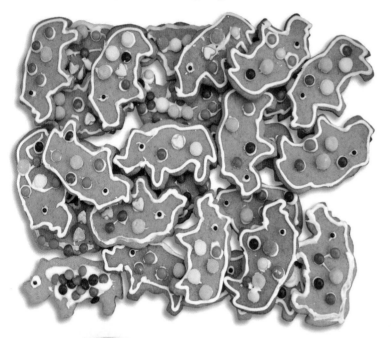

- ◆ **Mix dry ingredients** together in a bowl and **rub in** the margarine.
- ◆ **Add** beaten egg and syrup.
- ◆ **Knead** until it forms a stiff dough and the sides of the bowl are clean.
- ◆ **Roll out** thinly and **cut into rhino** and **ranger shapes.**
- ◆ **Place** shapes on large baking tray and **bake** at 180C for 10-15 minutes.
- ◆ **Cool** and **ice** with butter icing.

◆ **Decorate** your rhinos and rangers with sweets or cake decorations.

◆ **What** do think Alyssa and Rogan are going to do with their yummy biscuits? (see page 47).

Marshmallow rhino

Sweet treat - easy and fun to make. **No baking!**

Ingredients:
2 or 3 different size marshmallows,
edible colour spray or liquid food colouring,
black and white icing,
toothpicks.

Hi there!

- ◆ **To make the body – Stick** two large marshmallows together using a couple of toothpicks.
- ◆ **Attach** four small marshmallows on as **legs**, using half a toothpick each.
- ◆ **Join on** a marshmallow for the **head**, using a couple of half toothpicks.
- ◆ **Cut** out a **horn** and two **ear shapes** from a spare marshmallow.
- ◆ **Stick** them on with a little icing.
- ◆ **Paint** your rhino with a little dilute food colouring or **spray** it with edible colour spray.
- ◆ **When dry, pipe on** icing to make **eyes** and a **mouth**.

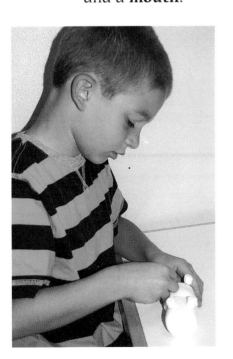

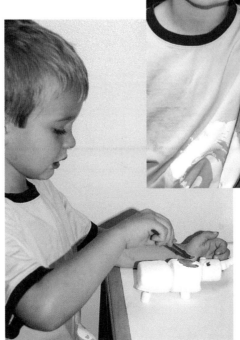

◆ If you want a **rhino to keep** – make it from **foam marshmallows**.

51

Colouring-in

Copy and **print out** these two pages
and then have fun **colouring** them in.

Rhino paper plate mask

Make this simple mask and become **a rhino** with **one** or **two pointy horns** or **display it** on the wall.

> **Need**: 2 paper plates or 1 paper plate and ice cream cones for horns, coin, scissors, pencil, paints or crayons, a piece of string or elastic.

- ◆ **Use** the back of the plate as it curves better to fit the face and is usually already grey.
- ◆ **Draw** in the mouth and eyes.
- ◆ **Cut** the second paper plate into **4 wedges** and use these to make the **horns** and **ears**.
- ◆ **Position** the **horn** or **horns** on the face and trace round the base. **Cut out** these circles slightly smaller and push through the horns.
- ◆ **Attach** ears.
- ◆ **Cut out** eye holes to peep through.
- ◆**Paint** the plate if you want to.
- ◆**Attach** string or elastic to the sides, as shown.

I can see you!

◆ **Now pretend you're a** *wild rhino!*

Rhino book marker

Great idea for a present!

Time for **folding** and **cutting fun**! Make this friendly rhino book marker.

Need: coloured or white thin card, stick on eyes, pencil, felt pens, paints or crayons, scissors.

◆ **Copy** this rhino book marker shape onto folded cardboard.
◆ **Cut out** book marker shape.
◆ **Colour-in** the rhino if you've used white card.
◆ **Stick** on two small white paper circles for the eyes or use stick on eyes.
◆ **Stick** the two sides of the horns together.
◆ **Pull** the sides of the face outwards slightly to give the head a shape.

◆ **While you're reading** your rhino will **stand** patiently on the table waiting for you!
◆ When you stop reading, **slide** the rhino **over** the **top of the page** with the legs on either side of the page, to **keep your place!**

Creating rhinos

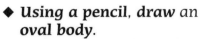

Draw me!
Draw me!

Drawing a rhino is **so easy**. Just practice these few simple shapes and in no time you'll have drawn your very own **Rhino**.

oval   cylinder   triangle

Need: Paper, pencil, felt pens, crayons or paints, erasure.

- ◆ **Using a pencil**, **draw** an **oval body**.
- ◆ **Make** a large **triangular head,** cutting off the point by the **mouth**.
- ◆ **Draw cylinders** for the **legs**.
- ◆ **Make** two **triangles** for the **horns**.
- ◆ **Sketch** in the **ear**.
- ◆ **Draw** the final **outline** in black felt tip. Remember to add in **eyes** and **mouth**.
- ◆ **Rub out** the pencil lines.
- ◆ **Colour-in** and **cut out** your rhino.

◆ **Stick** Rhino onto a **card** or **make a picture.** See page 61.

Playdough rhino

Need: Playdough or modeling clay, pencil or pointed object to make eyes and mouth.

Now take those same **shapes** you learnt in the drawing and make them out of **playdough** or **clay**. Combine them all to **create** a cute model **Rhino**.

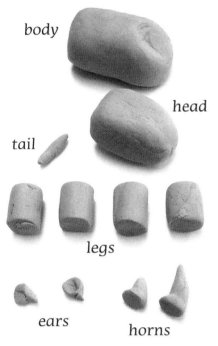

body

head

tail

legs

ears

horns

- ◆ **Make** an **oval body** and dent the top front for the head.
- ◆ **Make** a large **triangular head**.
- ◆ **Roll** a small sausage shape for a **tail**.
- ◆ **Roll** a larger sausage shape and cut it into **four cylinders**, one for each **leg**.
- ◆ **Make** two size **cones** for the **horns** and give them an upward curve.
- ◆ **Flatten** the little **ear balls** and pinch them at the bottom to make the **ear shape**.

Hi there!

- ◆ **Place** Rhino's **body** on top of his **legs**. **Stick** on his **tail**.

- ◆ Very carefully **stick on** the **head** and then the **horns** and **ears**.

- ◆ **Add eyes** and **mouth** by using the pointed object. Is he smiling?

57

Beach art

Next time you're at the **beach** have fun **creating a rhino.** It could be **small** or on the other hand, **really humongous,** so it would be visible from an airplane.

Some of the **things** you may find **on a beach** to add to your **rhino artwork**, depending on it's size.

ears

eyes

horns

A **sandy beach,** or a **sand pit,** is a lovely place to **draw rhinos** or **make** a **rhino sand sculpture.**

Use those same basic shapes from page 56 to create your rhino.

- ◆ **Wet** the sand slightly and **flatten** it.

- ◆ **For a sculpture – fill** the outline with piles of **sand.**

- ◆ **Draw the outline** of your rhino with your finger or a stick

- ◆ **Smooth** out the **sand** to make **rhino shape.**

◆ **Sit back** and admire your **work of art!**

Rhino inspired artworks

These **wonderful works of art** were created by people of all ages, worldwide, after being **inspired** by the **rhino**.

Hopefully you have also been enthused by the **rhino activity pages** and now it's time to have fun **making** your own **rhinos** – baking, drawing, painting, modeling playdough or even playing on the beach!

So many awesome things!

South Africa

Joel painting a beautiful game reserve for all his animals to live in.

New Zealand

White Rhino & Calf
Gordon Howard

Wild life artist, **Gordon Howard** was inspired as a young boy by the ancient rhino rock art in Zimbabwe.

Zimbabwe

World renowned mouth and foot painting artist, **Tom Yendell** and his wife **Lucy**, painted this amazing, colourful **Rosie the rhino** sculpture, as part of a **rhino fundraising campaign**.

England

This is Anna's cross-a-noceros!

South Africa

Maxine and **Kristin's** art used on an Anti-Poaching Vehicle.

South Africa

"please keep the rhino's safe"
– Maxine aged 6

"Dear Mr Poacher, please take this flower and leave my horn alone – see there behind me is my baby that I need to look after"
– Kristin aged 4

Soap stone carving of a rhino by an unknown **African artist**.

Zimbabwe

Robyn, Jess and **Joel** created lovely rhino **greeting cards** – all different.

Happy Birthday

North America

This is my **special** friend!

South Africa

I like this bead and wire one!

Arms full of **cuddly rhinos!** Above is **Alyssa,** with her very own '**crash of rhinos**' and many others kindly knitted and donated by **Sheelagh**, especially for Alyssa to sell.

Australia

South Africa

Grandpa Pete showing **Jack** how to make a rhino out of modelling clay.

61

Judy Maré

A special thank you to Margy Wakefield for sharing her happy childhood memories that inspired the Rhino story. Also to family and friends around the world and their children who helped me to bring this book to life.

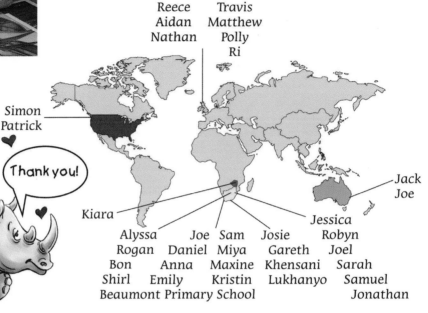

Reece
Aidan
Nathan

Travis
Matthew
Polly
Ri

Simon
Patrick

Thank you!

Jack
Joe

Kiara

Jessica

Alyssa   Joe   Sam   Josie   Robyn
Rogan   Daniel Miya   Gareth   Joel
Bon   Anna   Maxine Khensani Sarah
Shirl   Emily   Kristin Lukhanyo Samuel
Beaumont Primary School   Jonathan

Margo Branch, Bryony van Wyk and Aileen Edwards for all their expertise and constructive suggestions.
Linda Herud for taking such good care of rescued animals and her lovely photos.
Adele Lundie for the special rhino cover photo.
Gordon Howard, Peter Wakefield, Tom and Lucy Yendell www.amfpa.com for their works of art.

A huge thank you to the following organisations for their amazing photographs and the opportunity to share a little of the incredible work that they do. Find out more about them on their websites and please support them where you can.

Fact section
The David Sheldrick Wildlife Trust   www.sheldrickwildlifetrust.org
Save the Orangutan   www.savetheorangutan.org
Borneo Orangutan Survival Foundation   www.orangutan.or.id
Monarto Zoo, South Australia   www.zoossa.com.au
VulPro, vulture conservation program   www.vulpro.com
Save the Rhino International   www.savetherhino.org
Hoedspruit Endangered Species Centre   www.hesc.co.za
African Conservation Experience   www.conservationafrica.net
Blue Ridge Wildlife Center   www.blueridgewildlife.org

Activity section
EnviroKids Magazine, WESSA (Wildlife and Environment Society of South Africa) for allowing use of my tracks illustration.
SANParks Honorary Rangers who endorse Alyssa   www.sanparksvolunteers.org/alyssa-carter
Alyssa and her Save the Rhino's   www.savetherhinos.co.za
Nokana Safari Camp   www.nokana.co.za

NOTE:
The remaining pages have been intentionally left blank as **your special section of the book –** for artwork, notes or fotos. You could also stick the bottoms and sides of the pages together to **form a pocket,** in which to store treasures you collect or make.

Printed in Poland
by Amazon Fulfillment
Poland Sp. z o.o., Wrocław